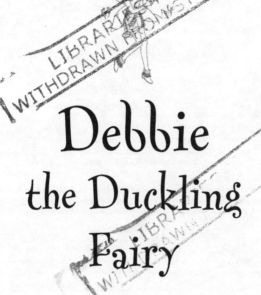

Debbie
the Duckling
Fairy

by Daisy Meadows

ORCHARD

www.rainbowmagic.co.uk

The Fairyland Palace

Farmhouse

Pond

Fluttering Fairyland Farm

Greenfields Farm

Greenfields House

Barn

Pond

Jack Frost's Spell

I want a farm that's just for me,
With animals I won't set free.
It's far too slow to seek each one.
Let fairy magic get this done!

With magic from the fairy farm,
I'll grant my wish – to their alarm!
And if I spoil the humans' fun,
Then Jack Frost really will have won!

Contents

A Happy Half Term

"It's so nice of your friends to invite me to the farm with you," said Rachel Walker.

Her best friend Kirsty Tate smiled. They were on their way to Greenfields Farm in the car with Mr and Mrs Tate. The farm was just outside Wetherbury, Kirsty's home town, where the two best friends

were spending the spring half-term
holiday.

"Greenfields Farm is so cool," Kirsty
said. "Mum and Dad have known the
owners for years, and they were really
happy to invite you along as well."

"Niall and Harriet Hawkins work
very hard," said Mr Tate. "They've been
planning to open the farm to paying
visitors for months."

"They were so pleased when we offered
to help them set up for the opening at
the end of this week," Mrs Tate added.

"The new visitors are bound to love
the little baby animals that have been
born this spring," said Kirsty.

"The babies are the ones I'm most
looking forward to seeing," said Rachel.
"I keep trying to decide which are my

favourite baby animals, but I never can."

The car started to bump down the lane towards the farm. The girls rolled the back windows down, and a chorus of birdsong flooded into the car.

"That's better than any car radio," said Mrs Tate. "What a beautiful sound."

"Look!" said Kirsty, pointing into the nearest field. "Look at all the animals. I can see cows… and sheep…"

"And there are some gorgeous horses over here," said Rachel, gazing out of the other window. "I wonder if we'll be allowed to ride them."

"I think we'll be too busy stroking the sweet little foals," said Kirsty.

The girls shared an excited smile as the car stopped outside the farmhouse. It was made of reddish bricks, and the door and windows looked freshly painted. There were cheerful yellow curtains in every window.

A tall woman with straight blonde hair strode around the side of the farmhouse and waved to them.

"That's Harriet," said Mrs Tate, waving back.

"You're just in time," said Harriet, smiling as they all got out of the car.

"I'm sorry to put you to work straight away, but we have an emergency. We have to mend a broken fence before one of the animals gets hurt on it, or escapes."

"That's what we're here for," said Mr Tate with a grin. "Lead the way, Harriet. We can unpack later."

"I'm so grateful that you're all here," said Harriet. "Come around the barn at the back of the farmhouse. Niall is just finishing the milking."

The scent of honeysuckle filled the air as Rachel and the Tates followed Harriet around the side of the farmhouse. Outside a small barn, a dark-haired

man was standing beside a cow, holding a bucket filled with milk.

"Hello, everyone," he said as they walked towards him.

"Welcome to the farm! Girls, this is Blossom. Would you like to say hello?"

Rachel and Kirsty felt very excited, but they made sure that they walked slowly, so they didn't startle Blossom. Soon they were patting and stroking her, and she was gently mooing. The girls thought that she was the nicest cow they had ever seen, with her soft nose and her big, shining eyes.

"I can see that you two love animals," said Harriet. "Would you like to go and see the new ducklings at the pond while we mend the fence?"

"That would be brilliant," said Kirsty.

"I'd love to!" said Rachel at exactly the same time.

Harriet pointed to a field on the right of the barn, while the girls jigged up and down in excitement.

"That's where the broken fence is," she said. "If you need us, you'll find us there. The pond is down that path."

She pointed to where a path wound along the edge of a different field. It disappeared between two large trees.

"The pond is just past those trees," said Harriet. "Enjoy watching the ducklings, and come back when you're ready for a big Greenfields Farm dinner!"

Rachel and Kirsty hurried along the path. The hedge that marked the edge of the field was full of colourful wild flowers.

"Red campions, foxgloves, celandines... I can't decide which ones I like best," Kirsty said, running her hand along the hedgerow as they walked.

"Let's pick some on our way back and put them in a jam jar in our room," Rachel said.

The girls held hands and walked through the trees that Harriet had pointed out. At once they saw a large pond sparkling in the sunshine, surrounded by tall reeds. Mother and father ducks lined the banks, resting in the sun while the tiny ducklings quacked and happily splashed in the water.

"Goodness, they are so loud," said Kirsty with a laugh. "I can't believe that something so small can make such a big noise."

But Rachel didn't reply, because she was gazing at the ducks' nest on the opposite bank of the pond.

"Look, Kirsty," she said in a low voice. "The nest is glowing."

The girls shared a thrilled smile, because they knew exactly what this meant. They were friends with the fairies, and they knew that the glow was magical. As they watched, the glow grew brighter and then a tiny fairy flew out of the nest and swooped across the pond.

Creatures in the Clouds

"Hurray, I found you!" the little fairy cheered.

She looped the loop over the noisy ducklings, who flapped their fluffy wings and quacked even more loudly. Her wings glimmered in the sunshine as she hovered in front of the girls.

"Hello," she said, smiling. "I'm Debbie the Duckling Fairy."

Debbie had ruffled light-brown hair with blonde tips and sparkling amber eyes. She was wearing a green T-shirt and a pair of blue shorts, and her gold necklace shone in the sunshine.

"I'm Rachel and this is Kirsty," said Rachel.

"Oh my, I know that!" said Debbie with a bubbling laugh. "I came here to

find you! A little bird told me that you were here, and I came to look for you straight away. We've had some new arrivals at the Fairyland Farm too. Would you like to come with me and see the baby animals?"

"Oh yes, please!" said the girls together.

They knew that the grown-ups wouldn't be worried. However long they spent in Fairyland, not a single moment would pass in the human world. Debbie lifted her wand and flew around the girls, trailing fairy dust behind her. She went faster and faster, until she was no more than a blur. The girls blinked and rubbed their eyes. When they looked again, they were hovering with pale, gossamer fairy wings, high in the sky, among big, fluffy white clouds.

"I'm so excited
that you're
here," said
Debbie,
who was
hovering
beside them.
"Welcome to the
Fluttering Fairyland Farm."

Rachel and Kirsty had to rub their
eyes again. In front of them, a large
green field was floating in mid-air. In the
far corner was a little cream-coloured
farmhouse, with a red roof and green
shutters on the windows. Next to the
farmhouse, a round pond glimmered
in the sunshine. There was a barn with
a curved roof, and stalls with space for
three ponies inside.

But none of the buildings was as wonderful as the animals that lived in them. Tiny ducks glided across the pond, and little pink pigs snuffled in the trough. Goats sprang across a little brook, and the sheep looked like tiny white clouds on the grass.

A farmer was standing outside the farmhouse, watching over the animals and smiling.

"That's Francis, the Fairyland farmer," Debbie explained, waving to him. "And there are the other Baby Farm Animal Fairies."

Three other fairies were playing with the farm animals. Debbie called to them, and they zoomed up from the magical farm at once.

"Welcome!" they said, gathering around their visitors and smiling. "We're so pleased you could come."

"I'd like you to meet Elodie the Lamb Fairy, Penelope the Foal Fairy and Billie the Baby Goat Fairy," said Debbie. "Together, we take care of the baby animals that are born each year, with the help of our magical baby animals."

"Come and meet Francis," said Elodie in a gentle voice.

Rachel and Kirsty flew down with the other fairies and landed beside Francis. He was wearing a yellow waistcoat and a checked hat, and he smiled from ear to ear when he looked at Rachel and Kirsty.

"I'm very proud to welcome you here at last," he said. "I've heard a lot about you from the fairies."

"It looks like a really happy farm," said Rachel, gazing around. "You must really love all your animals."

Francis nodded. "We have lots of wonderful animals here," he said. "And I have lots of visits from Debbie, Elodie, Penelope and Billie, because the magical baby farm animals live here too."

"Oh, you must come and meet Splashy!" said Debbie, bouncing up and down and clapping her hands together. "He's my magical duckling, and he's so sweet and funny."

Splashy was playing with the other

ducklings in the pond. Even though he was the same size as them, Rachel and Kirsty could tell instantly which one he was. His fluffy feathers shone with a tint of gold, and there was something extra special about the look in his bright eyes.

"He's adorable," said Kirsty. "I'd love to meet all the animals you have here."

"And I'd love to introduce them to you," said Francis. "Follow me."

Kidnapped!

The fairies and Francis led Rachel and Kirsty to a daisy-filled meadow. A little white lamb came bouncing over to them.

"It's as if she has springs in her legs!" said Rachel, laughing at the sight. "And look, she has the same tint of gold in her wool as Splashy."

"This is Fluffy, my magical lamb," said Elodie.

"She's adorable," said Kirsty, stroking Fluffy's soft coat.

Next they met Frisky the foal. Penelope had to coax him out of the little stall at first.

"He's a bit shy," she said, as Frisky snuggled into her arms.

"He's lovely," said Rachel in a gentle voice.

Soon Frisky was nuzzling Rachel's arm,

and she felt as if she had made a new friend.

"Come and meet Chompy," said Billie.

The magical baby goat made everyone laugh by trying to push his nose into Kirsty's pockets.

"He's very curious," Billie said.

"I don't mind," said Kirsty with a giggle.

Just then, Splashy came flapping out of the pond to join them, and everyone giggled as the magical babies wobbled and waddled around together on the bright green grass of the farm.

"There are plenty more animals to see," said Francis. "Come and meet the cows – there's a brand-new baby calf that I'm sure you'll love."

The fairies followed Francis towards the barn, leaving the magical babies playing. Inside, a little calf was standing beside his mother. He looked at the visitors and blinked his big, brown eyes.

"This is Toffee," said Francis in a soft

voice. "He's only one day old."

One by one, the fairies fluttered over to Toffee and stroked his brown coat. At first he was shy and pressed close against his mother, but after a little while he relaxed. Soon he was nuzzling the fairies and making happy, snuffly noises.

Suddenly, a rough cackle rang out across the farm. Toffee gave a jolt of shock and pressed against his mother again.

"I recognise that laugh," said Rachel in alarm.

Francis and the fairies zoomed out of the barn, and a horrible sight met their eyes. Jack Frost and three goblins were standing on the grass in the middle of the farm. Frisky was tucked under Jack's arm, and each of the other magical animals was under the arm of a goblin. Jack Frost was smiling his cruellest smile.

"Oh no!" cried Debbie.

"Stop, thieves!" Rachel called out.

Jack Frost gave another cackle of laughter.

"I don't take orders from silly little fairies," he stated.

"These animals do not belong to you," said Francis in a very stern voice. "Put them down at once."

Jack Frost replied with
a long, loud raspberry.

"Shan't," he
snapped. "My snow
goose and her baby,
Snowdrop, need
some friends. So
I'm going to make

my very own petting farm at my Ice
Castle, starting with these animals."

"You can't just take these animals,"
Penelope exclaimed. "They're *our* friends,
and this is their home."

Jack Frost ignored her and turned to his
goblins.

"Meet me at the petting farm," he
ordered. "Here's some magic to get you
there. I have to go and see my snow
goose now."

He disappeared in a bolt of blue lightning, but the three goblins looked at each other with disobedience on their faces.

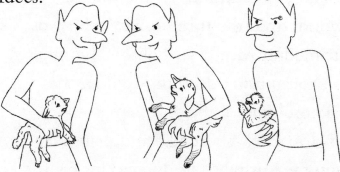

"They're glowing blue," said Rachel in astonishment.

"That's because Jack Frost has given them each a tiny bit of his magic," said Debbie.

"Goblins with their own magic?" said Elodie. "I don't like the sound of that."

"I want all the cuddles for myself," the goblin holding Splashy was saying.

"Me too," said the one with Fluffy in his arms. "But how can we keep the babies away from Jack Frost?"

"Let's go and hide in the human world," said the third goblin, who was struggling with a wriggling Chompy.

"You mustn't do that," said Kirsty. "Those animals belong here."

"Too late!" shouted the goblins. "You can't tell us what to do, and Jack Frost won't be able to find us when we hide away. We'll be the most famous goblins in Goblin Grotto."

They vanished in a flash of blue, taking the magical babies with them.

"We have to get back to the human world," said Debbie.

With a wave of Debbie's wand and a whoosh of fairy dust, the girls found themselves standing once again beside the pond at Greenfields Farm. Debbie was still with them, her eyes blazing.

"Poor Splashy will be so scared," she exclaimed. "That horrible Jack Frost — and those naughty goblins — how dare they steal our little friends away?"

"I'm sure Splashy knows that you will come and save him," said Rachel, trying to comfort the little fairy.

"It's not just Splashy I'm worried about," Debbie went on. "He helps me to look after ducklings everywhere and keep them out of trouble. Without him, I don't know how to take care of them all."

Just then, the girls noticed that there was a lot of noise coming from the pond. All the grown-up ducks were swimming around in circles and quacking loudly.

"Are they looking for something?" asked Kirsty.

"I can't see a single duckling," Rachel exclaimed. "This pond was full of them last time we were here. Oh, Kirsty, where are all the ducklings?"

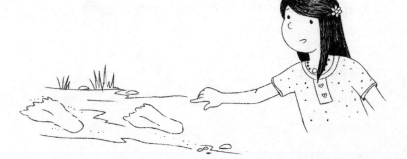

Woof or Quack?

"It's happening already," said Debbie, biting her lip. "Without Splashy by my side, ducklings all over the human world are going to get into trouble."

"Look over here," said Kirsty, peering at the soft mud on the bank of the pond and pointing. "Do these look like goblin footprints to you?"

Large footprints were leading away
from the pond and along the path to the
farm. Rachel and Debbie nodded.

"Well spotted," said
Debbie. "Let's
follow them."

"It'll be
easier to
follow
them if
we can
all fly," said
Rachel.

"Hide in the reeds, just in case anyone
comes along," said Debbie.

Rachel and Kirsty dived into the reeds,
and Debbie raised her wand. Soon,
the three fairies were zooming over
Greenfields Farm, their eyes fixed on the

goblin footprints below. The fields looked like a beautiful patchwork.

"Look, there are Mum and Dad," said Kirsty, pointing down to the field where the grown-ups were mending the fence.

Nearby, Blossom was grazing in the pasture outside her barn. The goblin footprints led the fairies past her and all the way to the farmhouse.

"I can hear puppies yapping," said Debbie, speeding up. "Perhaps something has upset the farmhouse dogs."

"Something or some*one*," said Rachel. "I'll bet it's someone green and grumpy. They've probably scared the puppies."

"But Niall and Harriet don't have any puppies," said Kirsty.

She and Rachel caught up with Debbie and they all landed in the yard. They were so small that the gaps between the cobbles seemed as wide as country lanes.

"Let's hide around the side of the farmhouse and turn back into humans," said Rachel. "We'll have a better chance of stopping the goblins if we are big again."

The yapping from inside the farmhouse grew louder, and Debbie quickly transformed the girls into humans again. She darted into Rachel's  pocket and the girls hurried into the farmhouse kitchen through the open door. They expected to see a basket full of playful puppies.

Instead, a crowd of fluffy little ducklings
surrounded them. They were yapping,
chasing their tails and chewing
everything in sight. There wasn't a single
quack to be heard or waddle to be seen.

"Oh my goodness, the ducklings are
acting like puppies!" Kirsty exclaimed.

Rachel clutched Kirsty's arm and
pointed at a group of ducklings over by

the sink. One of them had feathers that
glimmered with a tint of gold.

"Debbie, I think we've found Splashy!"
she said.

They heard a loud squawk,
and a goblin hurtled across
the kitchen towards Splashy.

"Come here!" he
screeched. "I want to
cuddle you!"

The other
ducklings
scrambled
sideways
as the
goblin dived among them. Splashy
yapped and bounded around in a circle
and the goblin crashed into the oven
door. He sat up, rubbing his head.

"I just want a cuddle," he wailed. "Splashy, don't run away from me. Come back!"

As he stood up and carried on chasing Splashy, Debbie flew out of Rachel's pocket.

"These poor ducklings are so confused," she said, her voice shaking as she called out to the goblin. "Please go away! I need Splashy back so the ducklings can start acting like ducklings again."

The goblin took no notice.

"Greenfields Farm can't open to visitors with ducklings that act like puppies," said Kirsty. "Please listen to us."

But the goblin carried on chasing Splashy around the kitchen, as the yaps of the ducklings grew even louder.

"He's too interested in Splashy to take

any notice of us at the moment," said Rachel. "We have to get Splashy back before he does. But how?"

"I've got an idea," said Kirsty. "If the ducklings think they're puppies, then let's treat them as if they really are. Every puppy I've ever met has loved to chew slippers. Debbie, could you magic one up?"

"Of course," said Debbie.

She flicked her wand, and a checked slipper appeared in Kirsty's hand. She waved it at Splashy.

"Come on, Splashy," she called. "Come and chew this lovely slipper!"

Goblin on the Cobbles

Splashy started running towards her, but then another duckling tugged the slipper out of Kirsty's hand. He dashed into a corner and started chewing the slipper in his beak.

"We need another plan," said Rachel. "What else do puppies like? Walks…

games… I know! How about a game of fetch? Debbie, could you magic up a dog toy?"

In a flash, Rachel was holding a blue rubber toy in the shape of a duck. It quacked when she squeezed it, which made all the ducklings turn to look. Rachel squeezed it again and then threw it across the room.

"Fetch, Splashy," she called.

Splashy ran after the toy, yapping in excitement. But the goblin spotted him and lunged forward. This time, he managed to catch the little duckling in his long, bony fingers.

"Got you," he said. "Now you're mine!"

He raced out of the farmhouse kitchen into the cobbled yard, clutching Splashy to his chest. Debbie zoomed after him.

"Come on," she called to Rachel and Kirsty. "We mustn't lose him this time."

The girls ran after the goblin, and all the other ducklings dashed after them. They scrambled between the girls' legs, making them stumble.

"They almost tripped us up!" said Rachel.

"Oh, that gives me an idea," said Kirsty.

She raced back into the farmhouse and came out holding the blue rubber toy. She squeezed it and the ducklings turned to look.

"Fetch," said Kirsty.

She threw the toy across the yard, and it landed beside the goblin's big feet. Yapping, panting and barking, the ducklings bounded after it. They bumped against and between the goblin's legs, knocking him this way and that. The goblin screeched, wobbled and fell head over heels into a muddy puddle. In the confusion, he let go of Splashy.

At once, Rachel ran to scoop up the
magical duckling. She held him gently in
her arms and turned to Debbie.

"Splashy!" cried the Duckling Fairy in
delight.

She flew to him with her arms held out
wide. As soon as she
touched him,
he shrank to
fairy size.
Quacking, he
snuggled up
to Debbie.

"He's back
to his old self,"
said Debbie,
cuddling him
and kissing his
fluffy feathers.

"So are all the other ducklings," said Kirsty.

She smiled as the little ducklings waddled out of the yard towards the pond, quacking at the tops of their voices.

"They're very noisy – whether they're being puppies or ducklings," said Rachel with a laugh.

The goblin was watching the ducklings waddle away too, and he looked very sad. Kirsty felt sorry for him.

"Are you feeling worried about what Jack Frost will say?" she asked.

The goblin gave an awkward little wriggle as he looked at Kirsty.

"Yes, a bit," he said. "I expect there will be a lot of shouting when Jack Frost finds out that he won't have Splashy at his petting farm. But most of all, I'm going to miss the sweet little ducklings. They're so soft and cuddly."

"You can always visit a pond and
see the ducklings splashing about," said
Debbie. "Ducklings love visitors. But you
have to promise that you will never again
try to take one away. They belong with
their mums and dads, just like Splashy
belongs with me."

"I promise," said the goblin, cheering
up at once. "I'm going to find a new
duckling pond to visit right now."

He ran off, and Rachel, Kirsty and
Debbie exchanged happy smiles.

"We did it," said Rachel. "Splashy
is safe, and the ducklings are back to
normal before the grown-ups noticed
anything was wrong."

"If we don't want the grown-ups to
notice anything, we'd better clean up the

farmhouse kitchen," said Kirsty, laughing. "Ducklings don't make neat and tidy house guests!"

The Mystery Cleaner

Laughing, they went back into the
farmhouse kitchen. It was covered in
feathers and the muddy prints of tiny
webbed feet. Bowls had been overturned,
cupboards and drawers had been emptied,
and tea towels had been chewed. The
contents of the kitchen bin were spread
across the floor.

Kirsty and Rachel started to roll up their sleeves, but Debbie stopped them with a smile.

"Leave this to me," she said, raising her wand.

Splashy perched on Kirsty's fingertip, and they all watched as Debbie waved her wand and spoke the words of a spell.

"Sweep feathers up, wipe mud away.
Reverse what happened here today.
Return each item to its place,
And do not leave a single trace."

Instantly, the kitchen was spick and span.

Debbie fluttered over to the girls and took Splashy into her arms again.

"Thank you for helping me to get him back," she said.

Splashy quacked loudly, and they all laughed.

"I think he's trying to say thank you too," said Debbie with her bubbling laugh.

"It's good to see you so happy again," said Rachel. "We loved meeting you both – and being able to help."

"I can't wait to tell Francis and the other Baby Farm Animal Fairies that Splashy is safe," Debbie went on. "I hope that we can find the other magical babies quickly too."

"We'll do everything we can to help," Kirsty promised.

"I'm going to take Splashy back to the Fluttering Fairyland Farm now," said Debbie. "I hope I'll see you both again soon. Goodbye!"

As the girls waved, Debbie disappeared back to Fairyland in a flurry of sparkling fairy dust. At that moment, the girls heard footsteps on the cobbles, and voices laughing. Then Mr and Mrs Tate came in with Niall and Harriet.

"Here you are," said Mrs Tate. "We

went to find you at the pond but all we saw were the sweet little ducklings."

"They're very cute," said Rachel. "I think they're my favourite farm babies."

"I thought that lambs were your favourite farm babies," said Kirsty.

"All farm babies are my favourites," said Rachel with a laugh. "I can't choose between them!"

Niall and Harriet were gazing around the kitchen with wide eyes.

"What on earth's happened here?" asked Harriet.

The girls exchanged a worried look.

Had Debbie's magic missed something?

"We left the kitchen in a real mess this morning," said Niall. "Who cleaned it up for us? Girls, was it you?"

"It wasn't us," said Kirsty truthfully.

"You must have elves," said Mrs Tate, laughing.

Harriet laughed too.

"I'll take all the help I can get," she said. "There are only a few days until opening day and we still have so much to do."

Soon, everyone was sitting around the big farmhouse table, tucking in to a delicious dinner.

"Why does working outside always make you so hungry?" asked Mr Tate, as he had his third helping.

Harriet looked at the girls.

"I'm glad you enjoyed meeting our ducklings," she said. "I hope that our visitors will love them too."

"Of course they will," said Rachel. "The ducklings are so sweet and so much fun. I could watch them splashing around for hours."

"It's really interesting to see them play together while their mums and dads watch," Kirsty added. "They're just the same as little children at the park."

"You know, Harriet and I would really like some help with the baby animals over the next few days," Niall said. "Would you two like to be in charge of looking after them?"

"Really?" asked Kirsty, her eyes wide. "Oh, yes please."

"We'd love it," Rachel added.

"That's decided then," said Harriet. "We'll show you what needs to be done in the morning."

As the grown-ups continued to chat, Rachel and Kirsty exchanged a secret glance. Looking after the baby animals sounded like the most delightful job on the farm.

"We've got three more animals to find before Greenfields Farm opens to visitors," Kirsty whispered to Rachel. "Looking after the animals here might help us to get the rest of the magical baby farm animals back from Jack Frost and the goblins."

"This is going to be an unforgettable half term," said Rachel. "A whole week of magical adventures and sweet baby animals. I can't wait!"

The End

**Now it's time for Kirsty and
Rachel to help...**

Elodie the Lamb Fairy

Read on for a sneak peek...

COCK-A-DOODLE-DOO!

Kirsty Tate and Rachel Walker sat up
in bed at exactly the same moment. For
a few seconds, they couldn't think where
they were. Then they remembered, and
shared an excited smile.

"You know you're on a farm when
a cockerel is your alarm clock," said
Rachel, bouncing out of bed. "Quick,
let's get dressed. I can't wait to say good
morning to all the animals."

This was their first full day at
Greenfields Farm, just outside Wetherbury,
where they were going to spend the

whole of the spring half term. The farm was owned by Harriet and Niall Hawkins, friends of Kirsty's parents, and they were getting ready to open it up to paying visitors at the end of the week. The Tates and Rachel had come to help them.

Kirsty slipped out of bed too, and threw open the yellow curtains. The walls of the farmhouse were so thick that the windowsill was big enough to sit on. Kirsty put the blanket from her bed on the sill, and then perched there, gazing out over the farm. She could see the barn where they had met Blossom the cow, and the trees that hid the sparkling duck pond. Over to the left she could see a green pasture, with sheep dotted around it like little puffs of cotton wool.

"It's going to be a lovely sunny day,"

said Rachel, joining her at the window. "This is perfect weather for working outside."

"I wouldn't mind rain or snow, as long as we get to spend the day with baby animals," said Kirsty with a smile.

Read **Elodie the Lamb Fairy** to find out what adventures are in store for Kirsty and Rachel!

Competition!

The Baby Animal Farm Fairies have created
a special competition just for you!

Collect all four books in the Baby Animal Farm series
and answer the special questions in the back of each one.

**The newborn calf in
this book is called**

— — — — —

Once you have all four answers, take the first letter from
each one and arrange them to spell a secret word!
When you have the answer, go online and enter!

We will put all the correct entries into a draw and select
a winner to receive a special Rainbow Magic Goody Bag
featuring lots of treats for you and your fairy friends.
The winner will also feature in a new Rainbow Magic story!

Enter online now at www.rainbowmagicbooks.co.uk

No purchase required. Only one entry per child.
One prize draw will take place on 30/06/2017 and two winners will be chosen.
Alternatively UK readers can send the answer on a postcard to: Rainbow Magic,
The Baby Animal Farm Fairies Competition, Orchard Books, Carmelite House,
50 Victoria Embankment, London, EC4Y 0DZ.
Australian readers can write to: Rainbow Magic, The Baby Animal Farm Fairies Competition,
Hachette Children's Books, Level 17/207 Kent St, Sydney, NSW 2000.
E-mail: childrens.books@hachette.com.au.
New Zealand readers should write to: Rainbow Magic, The Baby Animal Farm
Fairies Competition, PO Box 3255, Shortland St, Auckland 1140

Calling all parents, carers and teachers!
The Rainbow Magic fairies are here to help
your child enter the magical world of reading.
Whatever reading stage they are at, there's
a Rainbow Magic book for everyone!
Here is Lydia the Reading Fairy's guide to
supporting your child's journey at all levels.

Starting Out

Our Rainbow Magic Beginner Readers are perfect for first-time readers who are just beginning to develop reading skills and confidence. Approved by teachers, they contain a full range of educational levelling, as well as lively full-colour illustrations.

1

Developing Readers

Rainbow Magic Early Readers contain longer stories and wider vocabulary for building stamina and growing confidence. These are adaptations of our most popular Rainbow Magic stories, specially developed for younger readers in conjunction with an Early Years reading consultant, with full-colour illustrations.

2

Going Solo

The Rainbow Magic chapter books – a mixture of series and one-off specials – contain accessible writing to encourage your child to venture into reading independently. These highly collectible and much-loved magical stories inspire a love of reading to last a lifetime.

3

www.rainbowmagicbooks.co.uk

"Rainbow Magic got my daughter reading chapter books. Great sparkly covers, cute fairies and traditional stories full of magic that she found impossible to put down" – Mother of Edie (6 years)

"Florence LOVES the Rainbow Magic books. She really enjoys reading now" – Mother of Florence (6 years)

The Rainbow Magic Reading Challenge

Well done, fairy friend – you have completed the book!
This book was worth 5 points.

See how far you have climbed on the
Reading Rainbow opposite.

The more books you read, the more points you will get,
and the closer you will be to becoming a Fairy Princess!

How to get your Reading Rainbow
1. Cut out the coin below
2. Go to the Rainbow Magic website
3. Download and print out your poster
4. Add your coin and climb up the Reading Rainbow!

There's all this and lots more at
www.rainbowmagicbooks.co.uk

You'll find activities, competitions, stories, a special
newsletter and complete profiles of all the
Rainbow Magic fairies. Find a fairy with your name!